Special thanks to Michael Ford

For Arthur Leonard Chadwick

ORCHARD BOOKS

First published in Great Britain in 2017 by The Watts Publishing Group

1 3 5 7 9 10 8 6 4 2

Text © 2017 Beast Quest Limited
Cover and inside illustrations by Dynamo
© Beast Quest Limited 2017

Team Hero is a registered trademark in the European Union
Series created by Beast Quest Limited, London

A CIP catalogue record for this book is available from the British Library.

ISBN 978 1 40834 355 5

Printed in Great Britain

MIX
Paper from
responsible sources
FSC® C104740

The paper and board used in this book are made from wood from responsible sources.

Orchard Books
An imprint of Hachette Children's Group
Part of The Watts Publishing Group Limited
Carmelite House, 50 Victoria Embankment, London EC4Y 0DZ

An Hachette UK Company
www.hachette.co.uk
www.hachettechildrens.co.uk

TEAM HERO

REPTILE
REAWAKENED

ADAM BLADE

ORCHARD

MEET TEAM HERO ...

JACK

POWER: Super-strength
LIKES: Ventura City FC
DISLIKES: Bullies

RUBY

POWER: Fire vision
LIKES: Comic books
DISLIKES: Small spaces

DANNY

POWER: Super-hearing
LIKES: Pizza
DISLIKES: Thunder

... AND THEIR GREATEST ENEMY

GENERAL GORE

POWER: Brilliant warrior

LIKES: Carnage

DISLIKES: Unfaithful minions

CONTENTS

CONTENTS

CHANCELLOR REX gazed out of
the arched window of his chambers.
Under the moonlight glowed the
towers and battlements of Hero
Academy. In the dormitories, all the
students were sleeping, exhausted by
the recent battles. But sleep wouldn't
come to Chancellor Rex.

Not while a traitor lurked in their midst.

Every time he shut his eyes, the words flashed up in his mind.

GENERAL GORE IS COMING FOR YOU, CHOSEN ONE.

They'd found the message scrawled on the door of the North Wing dormitory. The Chosen One was Jack, the newest student to come to the academy. He was the answer to an ancient prophecy.

Darkness will rise and conquer light, unless the Chosen One joins the fight ...

But whoever had written the message was a servant of the underground realm of Noxx, and its leader General Gore. He would stop at nothing to invade the human world with his evil creatures. How could Rex even think of sleeping until they had rooted out the culprit?

Perhaps his powers could help ...

The Chancellor raised his hands. As a young man he'd been able to conjure visions of the future quite easily, but now he was nearing sixty years old, it was much harder. The visions weren't as clear, and faded almost as soon as they appeared.

The air between his palms blurred. An image began to form.

Smoke and fire. The ruins of factories. Chains, heaps of scrap and broken-down machinery. The ground was a black wasteland, broken up by rivers of lava.

"The land of Noxx," Rex muttered.

He felt a bead of sweat trickle down his temple, but kept his hands raised.

The smoke cleared. Through the shimmering heat he saw a gigantic cloaked figure clad from head to foot in black armour. The Chancellor recognised him at once.

General Gore. The enemy of all humans, who loves only power and cruelty.

In the vision, Gore raised a hand and beckoned through the shreds of smoke.

But what's this?

A small figure, wearing the bodysuit of a Hero Academy student, strode

towards Gore. Rex squinted, but the boy was cast in shadow. He paused before General Gore, then dropped to one knee.

"You are chosen," Gore said triumphantly. "Chosen by me."

"Jack?" the Chancellor mumbled.

The image vanished. With a groan of despair Rex dropped his hands, slumping into a chair.

What he had seen made no sense. Why would the Chosen One side with their deadliest enemy?

A siren shook the Chancellor from his thoughts.

"The armoury, sir," said a voice in

his ear. It was Eagle, the name of the Oral Response and Combat Learning Escort device hooked over his ear. *"Security breach."*

Rex stood shakily, grabbed the shimmering glove from his desk and slipped it over his hand. This plasma gauntlet was the only weapon Rex ever carried. He ran for the door, taking a lift down six storeys to the armoury.

As he emerged in the underground corridor, someone appeared from thin air. His heart skipped a beat until he saw it was only Ms Steel, using her teleportation power. The purple-haired teacher was carrying her laser lance, a two-metre-long staff with a pointed tip that glowed and hummed in the gloom. Worry lines etched her dark features as she looked to the closed armoury door.

"Ready?" she said.

Rex nodded. He raised his gauntlet, ready to fire. He placed his other hand to the scanner by the door, and it slid open.

Ms Steel burst through, lance raised, then stopped.

"There's no one here," she said.

Rex swept his eyes over the weapons stores. Energy cannons,

electro-shields, crossbows, plasma blades ... All seemed undisturbed.

Then he noticed that one cabinet door was slightly ajar. His heart plummeted.

"The shadow vials," he said, rushing forward.

Opening the door fully, he saw a shelf holding five vials made of thick green glass.

There should be six.

"No!" cried Ms Steel.

Chancellor Rex nodded. "I'm afraid so. The Noxxian spy has stolen the shadow."

When Noxx had last invaded, a

thousand years before, the forces

of good had managed to collect

some of the shadow of their realm.

They'd wanted to test it to discover

its properties — but it was far too

dangerous. Anyone who came into

contact with the shadow was taken

over by evil.

The enemy in their midst had a terrible weapon indeed.

Ms Steel looked horrified. "The spy could use the shadow to create more servants of Noxx!"

The Chancellor thought of all the innocent students sleeping above. They each had their own powers, which made them a formidable army. But until the culprit was caught, Hero Academy was just too dangerous — especially for Jack.

"I fear there is only one solution," Rex said. "We must leave Intrepid Island."

CHAPTER 1

EVACUATION

"I WONDER what this is all about," said Ruby, scooping her black curls into a ponytail. She and Jack were walking towards the main courtyard. Danny came a few paces behind, shouldering the small rucksack that contained the energy crossbow he'd kept after their fight with Zarnik.

"I have no idea," Jack replied. "Every day in this place is a surprise. I can't believe I've only been here a couple of weeks."

And what a fortnight it had been. Since the mysterious Ms Steel had invited Jack to the school, he'd learned that his scaly, super-strong hands didn't make him a freak after all. Every student at Hero Academy had a special gift — some could fly, some could breathe underwater, and others could control objects with just their thoughts. Ruby's orange eyes could shoot beams of flame hot enough to melt metal.

After a lifetime of not fitting in, Jack had finally found a place he belonged.

The students filing from the school buildings were wearing silver bodysuits, each with patches in the colour of their school house. Jack's patches were red, while Danny's were blue, and Ruby's yellow. Hawk, Jack's Oracle, was hooked over his ear. To anyone who didn't know, it looked like a small headset, but it was actually an advanced supercomputer. At his side hung the Shadow Sword, which he had used to close the portals to Noxx. He was the first to wield it in over a thousand years, leading Chancellor Rex to believe he was the Chosen One — the warrior destined to defeat General Gore once and for all.

Jack paused beside one of the school's towering fortress walls. Fossilised into the stone was the body of Raptrix, a lizard-like creature with a deformed human head and spike-covered back. Raptrix had been one of Gore's minions, frozen in rock since the last Noxxian invasion. Jack frowned.

"Guys," he said, "wasn't Raptrix's mouth closed before?"

Now the creature's long jaws were

slightly open, revealing needle-like
teeth.

"You might be right," said Ruby.
She stepped back suddenly. "Careful!
There's broken glass on the ground."

Jack looked down at the glinting

fragments, which were lying right beneath Raptrix. *Weird — how did they get here?*

"Maybe we should tell the Chancellor," said Ruby. "Hey, Danny — do you see this?"

Danny didn't respond. He was staring off into space.

"I thought his power was supposed to be super-hearing," muttered Ruby.

Danny blinked. "Pardon?" He shook his head in confusion, revealing large pointed ears.

Jack smiled, but it faded quickly. The sonic blasters used by the Noxxian warrior Chiptra and her flock of Noxxian terrawings had really messed with Danny's ears. The noise had been unbearable to Jack, but for Danny it must have been far worse. He'd spent the last three days recovering in the infirmary.

"Do you want me to get the school doctor?" Ruby asked.

"Er … no — I'll be fine, thanks," said Danny.

Chancellor Rex was standing on a platform in the middle of the courtyard as all the students gathered, muttering to each other. Other teachers lined up behind him: Professor Rufus, the squat, red-haired technology teacher who could see through walls; old Mrs Hindmarch, who apparently had the power to summon tornadoes; and several others whom Jack didn't know. All looked grim-faced as the Chancellor began to speak.

"Pupils of Hero Academy," he said. "You all know the threats we face. A Noxxian spy is loose on the island. Until we discover our enemy, it is not safe for you to stay here. All students will be going to a hostel in Ventura City."

Jack glanced at Ruby and Danny as gasps spread among the crowd. *Leave*

Intrepid Island?

Chancellor Rex raised a hand for quiet. "I and a few other teachers will remain here to carry out the search," he said. "For the rest of you, this is not a holiday. You will use the opportunity to train in a city environment, using your powers in secret among the people who live there. I remind you all that you are students of Hero Academy. Make us proud." He let the words sink in. "OK, to the boats!"

The students filed towards the cliff-top steps leading down to the bay. Many were chattering excitedly, but several, Jack noticed, were throwing glances his way. His cheeks reddened.

"This is all your fault, Beacon," said a voice Jack recognised. He turned to see Olly, a boy his age in a bodysuit with green patches.

"Leave him alone," said Ruby, standing between them.

"Or what?" said Olly. "You'll blast me with your eyes? I'd like to see you try." Olly's feet lifted off the ground. He smirked at them as he hovered in mid-air.

Jack tugged Ruby away. "It's not worth it."

"Or maybe *you* want a fight?" said

Olly, sneering. "I hear you're some sort
of strong man."

"We're on the same side," said Jack.

Olly swooped menacingly towards
him. "We're *supposed* to be," he said.
"But since you came here everything's
got worse. The Chancellor might think

you're the Chosen One, but everyone else just thinks you're a freak."

Jack felt the words hammer into his heart. *Beak the Freak*. That was what the kids at his old school had called him.

Chancellor Rex appeared on the battlements and Olly backed up.

"What's going on down there?" the Chancellor called.

"Er … ah … we were …" Olly stammered.

"We were just talking about Ventura City, Chancellor Rex," said Jack. He didn't like Olly, but he didn't like telling on people either.

"Well, there'll be time for that on the boats," said the Chancellor sternly. "Get moving, all of you."

They set off for the shore. As he followed his friends, Jack's eyes were drawn to Raptrix one last time. He was more certain than ever that its jaws had been closed before. But stone couldn't move, could it? Surely he was just imagining things.

Something blurred in the corner of his vision. He was startled by Ms Steel appearing out of thin air beside him.

"Sorry," she said.

"That's all right," said Jack. "I'm getting used to it."

Ms Steel's face turned serious. "Listen, Jack. You must be especially careful while this spy is at large. Don't go anywhere alone."

Jack chewed his lip, remembering what Olly had said. "Maybe it would be safest if everyone steered clear of me."

"All heroes need friends, Jack." Ms Steel gave him one of her mysterious smiles, then vanished.

The jetty was lined with several sleek powerboats. Jack boarded with the others and the boats roared in convoy from the sheltered cove. They surged and bounced through the mist,

and soon they were on open water.
Jack gazed out, deep in thought.
Clearly, Ms Steel and Chancellor Rex
believed in him. But what if he *wasn't*
the Chosen One? What if they'd got
the prophecy wrong?

Soon the skyscrapers of the city rose into view. Students pointed excitedly and Jack's pulse quickened. He'd lived in Ventura City all his life. He wondered if he'd get a chance to see his parents.

I probably won't have time, he thought. *Anyway, what could I tell them?*

As far as his mum and dad were concerned, Hero Academy was just a special boarding school — one that would cater for Jack's gift and where he wouldn't feel different. They had no idea that its real purpose was to train heroes to keep the earth safe.

Since he'd joined the Academy, Jack had discovered that the students were sworn to secrecy about General Gore and his Noxxian army.

As the boat surged through the choppy water, a long black shape drifted alongside it. Jack jerked back, his heart racing.

He turned to Ruby and Danny. "There's something in the water!"

His friends peered over the side of the boat. Ruby looked puzzled. "I can't see anything," she said.

"Me neither," said Danny.

Jack looked again. He frowned. Whatever he'd spotted was gone.

"Weird," he said. "Can you hear anything, Danny?"

Danny pushed back his dark hair to reveal his bat-like ears again. "I don't think so," he said. "Just normal sea noises."

Jack stared at the water again. First Raptrix seemed to have moved, now this. Was he imagining things?

"Any idea what it could be, Hawk?" he asked his Oracle.

"Several species of shark are known to live in the Ventura Bay area," said Hawk enthusiastically. *"They're quite harmless – as long as you don't decide to dip your toes over the edge."*

But Jack couldn't shake the unease that tugged at him. He thought of Ms Steel's words of warning.

The Noxxian spy is out there, he thought. *I've got to be on my guard.*

CHAPTER 2

STEALTH TRAINING

THE ACADEMY boats moored up at the furthest jetty in Ventura City Port, away from the expensive yachts and huge freight ships. Here, there were only a few rusting containers stacked on the quayside.

Ms Steel appeared at the end of the jetty. Jack wondered if she'd teleported herself all the way from Intrepid Island.

She handed out chunky utility belts to each student.

"These are stealth packs," Miss Steel said. "They will allow your bodysuits to help you blend in. Inside them, you'll also find climbing equipment and other items. The first task is for you to find your way, in pairs, to the museum in the centre of the city."

The museum was the place where Jack had stopped a careering, out-of-control taxi with just his hands. A few minutes after that, Ms Steel had found him and invited him to join

Hero Academy. *It already seems like a lifetime ago*, he thought. He looked inside his pack and saw grappling ropes and suction gloves for climbing.

As the other students started pairing up, Ruby nudged Jack and gestured towards Danny. Their friend was again staring aimlessly. His skin was paler than ever against his dark hair.

"I'm worried," she said. "He's not himself."

"I'll look out for him," said Jack. "Hey, Danny — you want to team up with me?"

Danny nodded and drifted over.

"I'll go with Ellie," Ruby said, and

went to join a small girl with hair so fair it was almost white.

When everyone had paired up, Ms Steel said, "The Academy teachers will be scattered throughout the city. The aim is not to be spotted. If we see you, you've failed."

Jack groaned. "That's not fair! Ellie can turn invisible!"

Ellie grinned. "Now you see me," she said, then faded away before his eyes. "Now you don't," came her voice from thin air.

Ms Steel smiled. "Remember, everyone — the invisible can be seen, and the visible can be unseen."

Ruby frowned. "That doesn't make any sense!"

Ms Steel winked. "Off you go!"

Jack looked down at his bodysuit and the Shadow Sword hanging at his side.

"We won't fit in looking like this," he said. "Everyone will think we're going to a fancy dress party. Can you help, Hawk?"

"Since you are wearing a stealth pack, I certainly can. May I ask what look you would like?" asked Hawk.

"You give fashion advice?" said Jack doubtfully.

"Well, I suppose that's one way of

putting it," said Hawk.

"Erm, normal kid look, I guess."

A slight warmth passed over Jack's skin and the next moment he found

himself wearing jeans and a hoodie. The clothes felt just the same as his bodysuit, and Jack realised they were purely an illusion.

"Wow — that's ..."

"Practical and yet stylish," said Hawk proudly. *"You're most welcome."*

One by one, the other students morphed into different clothing, and soon they looked like an ordinary school group. Outside the wharf building, they began heading in different directions.

"Good luck," said Ruby, setting off with Ellie.

Jack turned to see where Danny

had got to. His friend was leaning against a boathouse, shoulders slumped.

"Sure you're up to this?" Jack asked.

"Of course," said Danny, straightening. His Oracle, Owl, had made him look like he was wearing tracksuit bottoms and a long-sleeved T-shirt. "Owl says the fastest route to the museum is by the underground train network."

"There are bound to be teachers there," said Jack. "I know a better way. I grew up in this part of the city, remember? Follow me."

Jack led Danny through the

streets to a shopping centre. It was a Saturday morning, so Ventura City was still quiet, with just a few families and tourists around. As they passed the shops, Jack kept his eyes peeled for teachers. They might well be in disguise too, so he had to stay sharp. Danny was lagging behind already, though. His lips were moving, like he was talking to himself.

What's wrong with him? As soon as this mission was over, Jack would speak to Ms Steel. Danny was clearly too ill to be taking part in training.

They followed an alley into winding streets. It was still early, and most of the restaurants weren't open yet. Jack thought he saw a flash of orange hair ahead. *Professor Rufus?* He ducked into a doorway with Danny. As he peeped out, the figure had gone.

"Danny," he said, "can you hear anything?"

Hugging his arms around himself, Danny shook his head. "Too many voices," he said. "I can't fix on any one sound."

Jack pursed his lips. If they moved into the open here, a teacher might see them straight away. He thought back to a few days after he arrived at Hero Academy, when he'd spent an afternoon trying out Hawk's different functions, and had another idea.

"Hawk, give me heat signature analysis," he said.

"Coming right up," Hawk replied.

A faint whir sounded by Jack's ear as the Oracle flipped a visor over one eye. Jack scanned the street, looking

for bodies. Someone was behind a lorry at the far end, very still — someone short. It had to be Professor Rufus.

"We need to find another route," Jack said. "Let's double back."

"OK," said Danny, his voice a croak.

Danny was pale and breathing hard by the time they reached the tall apartment blocks in the east of the city. The route was longer, but Jack figured there'd be fewer teachers likely to be lying in wait. They passed through a small park. As they got to the far side, Jack felt a prickle across the back of his neck. He spun round, but no one was there apart from Danny.

"Can you hear anything unusual?" Jack asked.

Danny nodded. "Underground, yes. I've been hearing it since we arrived." He stumbled, and Jack caught him. "I can't get it out of my head."

Jack looked at his friend. Danny's eyes were bloodshot and he was shivering. Jack glanced around and realised they weren't actually that far from his parents' house. He knew they'd ask questions, and Chancellor Rex might not agree with his plan, but Danny was getting worse, fast.

"Come on," he said. "Let's get you some help."

53

Putting Danny's arm over his shoulder, and using his super-strength, he supported his friend's weight with ease as they walked along the familiar streets to an apartment block. He pointed to a set of blue curtains on the ninth floor.

"That's where my parents live," he said. "My mum's a paramedic. She'll take a look at you."

"There's nothing she can do," said Danny, trying to pull away.

Jack kept a grip on his friend's arm. "Don't be silly. You can barely stand."

Suddenly something ploughed into them, smashing them both to the

ground. Jack felt a cold wind whip past, then it was gone.

He gasped. "What was that?"

His heat visor wasn't picking up anything, but he didn't need Hawk to tell him that something was out there — something big and strong, and completely invisible.

CHAPTER 3

KIDNAP

JACK STARED around him. A tree branch beside the apartment block moved. A few leaves scattered to the ground. By one of the second storey windows, a wet patch appeared — a three-toed footprint. Then another. Soon there was a trail heading right up the wall. Something was climbing the side of the building.

Towards my parents' place!

"Quick!" he said. "We've got to follow!"

Jack fished in his stealth pack and found the suction gloves.

"I don't know if I'm strong enough," said Danny, his voice a whisper. He was still sitting on the ground.

Jack was torn. He didn't want to leave his friend, but he couldn't abandon his parents either.

He heaved Danny to his feet and pushed him into a doorway. "Stay here," he said. "Keep out of sight."

Jack looked up at the side of the

building. When he started climbing, people would see.

"Hawk, is there a way to camouflage me against the brickwork?"

"Piece of cake," the Oracle replied.

Jack saw the colour of his clothes shift to a pattern almost identical to the bricks. He grinned and leapt up on to the wall. The suckers on the gloves gripped tight.

He began to climb, bracing against the wall with his feet and reaching up, channelling the power of his super -strength. At the third floor, he looked down. If he slipped now, the fall would probably kill him. The slimy trail above was getting closer to his apartment. Jack powered on faster, hand over hand, practically running up the vertical surface.

He heard the smash of glass, and curtains whipped from the broken window. Whatever the invisible thing was, it had got inside.

Then he heard a scream.

"Mum!" he cried. "Hold on!"

He scrambled over the sill, and hurled himself into the living room, feet crunching on broken glass covering the carpet. His mum and dad were hugging each other in the doorway leading to the kitchen.

"Jack!" said his dad, squinting at him. "Your clothes …? How did you …"

Jack looked down and Hawk made his bodysuit look like ordinary clothes again. Then he peered around the room. The air was cold — colder than

it should have been. It was the same intense chill he'd felt outside. He drew the Shadow Sword.

His mum gasped. "What's going on, Jack?" she said.

"There's something in here with us," said Jack. "Don't move."

Suddenly the front door exploded inwards and Danny stood there, energy crossbow levelled. Jack's parents cried out in alarm.

"This is Danny," Jack said quickly. "My friend from school."

"I took the lift," Danny said, his forehead soaked with sweat.

Jack felt the chill rush past once

more, then heard a horrible hiss. He spun round and grabbed at empty air, but his hands gripped something scaly. He clung on, feeling it thrash. Then something slammed into the side of his head and he lost his grasp, smashing into a bookshelf.

"Mum, Dad — run!" he said, through a wave of dizziness.

Just as they started to move, something fell on top of them. Jack struggled to understand what he was seeing. It was like some sort of see-through sack — a bubble of slime. His parents both opened their mouths to cry out, but the sound was muffled.

They struggled for a moment, then vanished.

"Mum!" cried Jack. He raised the sword to attack the invisible enemy but paused. *What if I hurt them?*

He heard a hiss and a cackle and a quiet voice growling. "Master will be pleased."

Danny was swinging the crossbow back and forth, clearly unsure where to aim. He jerked back as the weapon was knocked from his hands. With a shout of pain, he was sent flying over a side table, landing in a heap on the floor. Jack heard the rasps of their enemy's breathing and the thud

of its steps heading for the door. The
kidnapper was escaping.

Jack grabbed a vase of flowers
from the coffee table and hurled it
after the sounds. The vase seemed
to explode in mid-air, the sprinkling
water revealing a creature with a
broad, scaly back lined with spikes
disappearing through the door.

Jack wanted to follow, but he had
to help his friend.

"Danny?" said Jack, kneeling at
his side. Danny lay on the floor, his
crossbow a few metres away. His
eyelids fluttered and he tried to sit up
before sagging back.

"Stay still," said Jack. "I'll contact Ms Steel for help."

"No," mumbled Danny, eyes wide with fear.

Jack noticed his arm was tucked awkwardly behind his back.

"You're hurt!" said Jack. "Hawk, Owl, can you change our suits back to normal so I can see where he's hurt?"

But Danny struggled, trying to keep the arm hidden. Gently, Jack prised it out to find that Danny's sleeve had ripped. His arm looked very strange indeed — covered in a black coating. The skin beneath was bone-white, but the veins pulsing under his skin were

black, as if filled with oil instead of blood …

Or shadow.

Noxxian shadow.

"What's happened?" Jack asked.

Danny's face was full of shame and fear. "It's me," he said quietly. "I'm General Gore's spy."

CHAPTER 4

COLD BLOOD

JACK FELT as though he'd been punched in the gut. His eyes travelled up and down his friend's infected arm.

"It happened that day by the portal in the school courtyard," Danny explained. He looked down, as if he couldn't bring himself to meet Jack's eyes. "One of the Noxxian shadows touched me. I didn't say anything, because I hoped it would be OK."

Jack swallowed. He remembered the fight against Zarnik and his centipede minions, and the lashing shadows that had erupted from the portal. Chancellor Rex had warned them all to stay away from it, but Danny must have been hit.

"But I wasn't OK at all," Danny went on. "I started to have blackouts, dizziness and cold sweats."

"So it wasn't the damage from the sonic blasters making you ill?"

Danny shook his head. "No, it was the voices. In my mind. Not all the time. But when they came, I was powerless. They made me ... do things."

Jack shot a look towards the door. With every second, his parents were in more danger. But he needed to know what General Gore was up to, and Danny might be able to tell him.

"What things?" he asked.

Danny looked close to tears. "They made me tell General Gore about the Shadow Sword. And it was me who painted the threat on the dormitory door. I ... I stole too." He covered his face with his arm.

Jack put his arm on his friend's

shoulder to comfort him. He knew Danny was brave and loyal. "Don't worry. We'll talk to Chancellor Rex. He'll know what—"

"No, please don't," said Danny. "They'll expel me! I'll have to go back to normal school. I'll lose my friends, you and Ruby ... I'll lose everything!"

Jack didn't know what to say. It was possible Danny was right. Once the Chancellor found out, he might kick Danny out of Hero Academy. Or worse. What if there wasn't a cure?

Jack pushed the dark thought away. "We'll find out how to make you better," he promised.

A flicker of a smile passed over Danny's pale features. "Really?"

Jack nodded. "But first, we need to track down my parents."

Danny managed to stand up. "I think I know what's taken them." He looked down at his feet. "Raptrix."

Jack remembered the statue fossilised into the wall of the school and his throat went dry. "He's come to life?" he said.

Danny nodded. "I stole a vial of shadow from the armoury and poured it over him. I didn't want to, but the voices made me ..."

Jack's blood ran cold. He recalled

the broken glass beneath the fossil; its terrible jaws. And the shape that had slid beneath the boat on the way over to the city.

Not a shark at all.

Despair crept over Jack. "He must have heard me talking about my parents. I led Raptrix right to my home!"

"And now he must be taking them to General Gore," said Danny. "Jack, I'm so sorry."

What does Gore want with my parents?

Jack ran to the door, where the moist footprints had already vanished. He swept into the lift, followed by Danny, and hit the button for the ground floor. When the doors finally opened again at the bottom level, they charged out into the open courtyard in front of the building. Several paths and roads led away, and there was no telling which way the kidnapper had fled.

Danny staggered out behind him, panting. "Jack, wait!" he said. "Raptrix can make himself invisible whenever he wants — I saw him do it when he came back to life. How can we find Raptrix if we can't see him??"

Jack felt utterly helpless. Ventura

City was enormous — even with the whole school looking, they might never be able to locate Raptrix.

Unless ...

What was it that Ms Steel had said? *The invisible can be seen ...*

Jack frowned. "Hawk, can you set my visor to detect cold as well as heat?"

"I thought you'd never ask," said Hawk.

The visor over Jack's eye buzzed and the view changed to tones of blue. He turned a full circle, desperately searching. A shape like some sort of prehistoric lizard was slithering off down the road, a bulging sack over its shoulder. In the distance, through a gap in the apartment blocks, Jack saw a huge suspension bridge hanging from steel cables.

"There!" cried Jack. "Raptrix is

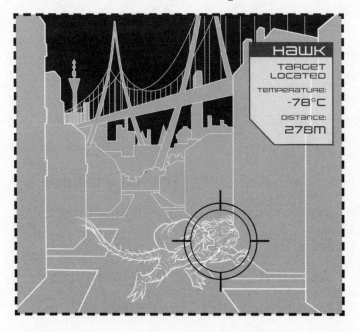

heading for the river."

Danny was bent double, coughing. "I can't go any further ..."

"Yes, you can!" Jack said, looping Danny's arm over his shoulder once more. Together they half-ran, half-stumbled after the fleeing Noxxian, before Jack decided to pick up Danny completely, charging through the streets. For one panicked moment, Jack thought he'd lost track, but then the lizard shape appeared once more, lumbering between two buildings a block up.

When they reached the main road, Raptrix was already climbing a ramp on to the bridge. Jack hurried after the creature, Danny still slung over his shoulders. Cars beeped and swerved as Jack ran across the busy street.

Lifting Danny was no problem, but running ten blocks had left Jack's lungs burning. Stumbling to the far side of the road, he saw Raptrix had stopped halfway across the bridge, standing over the edge, the sack clutched in his claws.

Though Raptrix was still mostly camouflaged, Jack was close enough to get a much better look at him. His enemy had a long slender tail covered

in spikes. His body was scaly and
muscular; his hind legs were stubby
but powerful; and his foreclaws were
hooked like talons. But his head was
almost human, with a jutting jaw, and

streaks of knotted hair hanging from a balding dome. The creature had no lips or nose — just slashes in his face. He was looking down into the water.

Jack followed his gaze and

shuddered. The water beneath the bridge was churning with a swirling current, a narrow funnel sinking into the middle of the river.

"Is that what I think it is?" mumbled Danny.

Jack nodded, eyes trained on the

whirlpool, and the shadows that licked within.

"A portal to Noxx," he said. "I think that's where Raptrix is taking my parents!"

CHAPTER 5

AERIAL ASSAULT

HOW COULD they even get close? As soon as they were up at the bridge level, Raptrix would see them coming.

And when he does he might drop Mum and Dad into the water!

But what else had Ms Steel said?

The visible can be unseen.

Jack had thought she was just

talking about Ellie, but as he looked up, he realised there was another way to reach Raptrix. *The bridge cables ...*

He pointed at the steel wires supporting the bridge. "Danny, if we can get up there, we can attack Raptrix from above."

His friend looked doubtful. "Jack, I don't have the strength to climb."

Jack looked at him, shivering and sweating, and hunched over. *He's right. I could carry him on my back, but it would only slow me down.*

"OK, stay hidden," Jack said. He hated leaving Danny, but his friend was safest out of the way.

Danny crouched at the bottom of a set of maintenance steps leading up to the bridge and Jack began to climb the nearest steel cable. It was as thick as his wrist, made of coiled wires. Jack placed each hand with care, trusting in his strength. A few cars had slowed on the road, with people winding down their windows to look.

That's not what I need, thought Jack. *They'll draw attention to me.* "Hawk, can you disguise me please?"

"I would be glad to! As part of the bridge, perhaps? Or—"

"Anything," said Jack, "just hurry!" Immediately his clothing shimmered pale blue to match the sky beyond.

Raptrix seemed focused on the portal, which was growing wider all the time. Jack wondered how long it would be until he jumped in, letting the portal suck him through to Noxx.

I'll never see my parents again!

He climbed faster, gripping with his knees and hauling himself up with his faintly glowing scaly hands. The wind picked up the higher he went, threatening to pluck him off the cable and send him plummeting into the traffic far below. Jack's heart thundered as he saw Raptrix crouching, ready to jump.

"Hey, slimeball!" came a voice.

It was Danny, stumbling along the side of the bridge, straight towards Raptrix. He moved with hobbling steps, clutching the rail that ran along the edge.

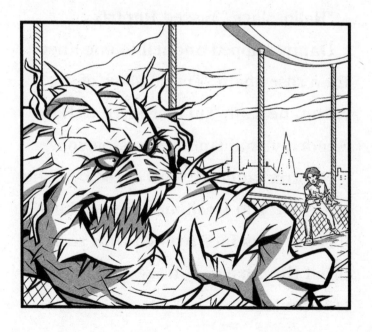

He's causing a distraction! Jack realised. With a rush of gratitude towards his friend, he shuffled further into position along a cable. Now he was almost directly over Raptrix's head.

"Hello, slave," hissed Raptrix.

Danny tripped and fell to one knee, then rose again. "I'm no slave of Noxx," he said. "I'm a student of Hero Academy, and I'm here to stop you."

Raptrix laughed. "You're too late," he sneered. "You freed me — remember?"

Danny, his face twisted with pain, lifted the crossbow. It swayed from side to side.

"I hope your aim is good." Raptrix smirked. "Wouldn't want to hit these two." He hoisted the squirming sack in front of him, a broad grin revealing his pointed teeth.

Jack held his breath, filled with horror. Danny was struggling even to keep the crossbow aloft. Finally, with a groan, he dropped it and collapsed.

Jack jumped from the wire, slamming into Raptrix's scaly back. The Noxxian spun around, foreclaws trying to grab at him. Grunting, the creature snagged Jack's tunic and hurled him off. Jack rolled across the tarmac. When he stood again, Raptrix had some sort of blaster in his hand. "So much for the Chosen One!" he said, and pulled the trigger.

Jack ducked as a ball of slime burst from the barrel. It splatted on to the bridge behind him. A bitter smell filled his nostrils, and Jack saw one of the metal cables melting into smoke.

Acid slime!

He drew the Shadow Sword and charged. The first swipe missed, but the second severed one of Raptrix's claws. The slime-gun arced through the air as Raptrix roared in pain. The sack dropped into the road and Jack heard the cries of his parents within.

Jack was about to swing the sword again, when something rushed up to his left. *Raptrix's tail!* It thumped into Jack's midriff. He crumpled, the wind knocked from his lungs.

"Danny, help me!" he cried.

GRAARR!

But as he turned to look for his friend, his eyes met a horrible sight. Danny was squirming on the ground, his tunic ripped open at the back to reveal bulges under his darkening skin. He rolled on to all fours, his fingernails lengthening like claws and digging into the surface of the road. His face twisted with agony as it changed, skin turning to leather. His bloodshot eyes stared at Jack, pleading.

"There's nothing you can do for him now," said Raptrix. "Your friend is becoming one of us."

The creature plucked up the bulging

slime sack and dangled it over the edge of the bridge. Inside, Jack's mum let out a panicked wail.

"No!" he shouted. First his friend, now his parents. His enemies had taken everything.

"Got your attention, have I?" said Raptrix. "Enough games. Drop your weapon and come to me."

Jack suddenly understood. "It's me you want, isn't it?"

Raptrix snorted. "Of course." He jerked the sack. "These pathetic humans mean nothing to my master. He'll just throw them into the fighting pits for sport. He wants the Chosen

One. Hand yourself over, and I will let them go."

Jack took a deep breath. He could see from Raptrix's steely gaze that he was without mercy.

I don't have a choice. It's my parents or me.

"OK," he said. "I'll come with you."

Raptrix grinned. "Throw aside the Shadow Sword."

Jack did as the creature said, leaving himself defenceless.

"And come closer," said Raptrix.

Jack stepped forward.

"Gore was right about you," said Raptrix. "He said you were a fool." He looked over the side of the bridge. "The portal is ready."

"Release my parents," said Jack. "That was the deal."

"With pleasure," Raptrix replied.

Then he dropped the sack into the water.

CHAPTER 6

DEATH MISSION

"*NO!*" YELLED Jack. He ran to the edge of the bridge. The sack splashed into the river. Almost at once, the current snatched it up, dragging it towards the whirlpool.

Jack didn't think. A split second later, he vaulted over the railings and dived towards the water far below.

The cold grabbed him like an icy fist. All he saw was bubbles. He kicked and thrashed, and soon his head burst through the surface. He took great gasps of breath. The sack was being sucked ever closer to the whirlpool's edge. If he didn't act fast, his parents might well drown before they even made it to Noxx.

Jack struggled through the water towards them. He managed to grab the sack in one hand, and with the other, he hauled himself away from the portal. But the water swirled powerfully. Even with his super-strength he wasn't getting anywhere.

His shoulders began to burn as he fought a losing battle against the pull of the whirlpool.

"Don't panic, Jack," shouted Raptrix from above. "Soon you will warm yourselves beside the lava fires of Noxx!"

"Never!" Jack cried.

He heard Raptrix yell, then saw him smashed aside. At the edge of the bridge, Danny appeared — except he barely looked like Danny any more. His skin was mottled with shadowy patches. His arms had grown long and spindly, and from his back sprouted huge leathery wings. He

gripped the side of the bridge with his new talons.

"Danny!" Jack yelled, still fighting the tug of the water. "The Shadow

Sword! I need it to close the portal!"

Danny gazed down, and a long black tongue slithered from his lips. Then he backed away from the bridge's edge. *He can't hear me!*

As Danny vanished from sight, Jack's hopes vanished with him.

His arms burned as he and his parents were dragged towards the edge of the portal. "I'm sorry," Jack cried, kicking with all his strength. "I can't fight the whirlpool any longer."

Something landed with a splash nearby. Jack's heart leapt as he saw the black shape of the Shadow Sword. *Danny did it!* Jack reached out his free hand, and his fingers found the hilt. He swung the blade and sliced through the top of the sack. His parents spilled out into the water, clutching each other.

"Swim!" Jack shouted. "Make for the shore!"

"Jack!" spluttered his father. "What's going on?"

His mother's lips were blue from cold already.

"Oh no!" she cried, pointing up.

Jack saw two bodies flailing in mid-air. One was Danny, wings flapping wildly. He had his talons jammed into Raptrix's shoulder. The creature snapped with his jaws and lashed with his tail.

I've still got to close the portal ...

Jack rolled on to his back, letting the whirlpool take him. He knew his timing had to be perfect.

As the water whipped him round in ever tighter circles, he angled the shadowy blade downwards. Just as he felt himself dropping into the black abyss, he rammed the sword into the depths of the spinning current.

Almost at once, he felt the water's grip loosen. The whirlpool slowed and the portal at its centre began to shrink. Jack swam to his parents' side.

Above, a terrible screech pierced the air as Danny sank his talons deeper into Raptrix's scaly flesh and furled his wings around his enemy. Locked together and unable to stay aloft, the two began to drop through the sky ...

Straight towards the closing portal.

Jack could only watch as the two creatures of Noxx hit the water and disappeared. A second later, the portal was gone.

Jack stared at the calm surface of the river, realising with a shuddering breath just what Danny had done. He had dragged Raptrix through the portal with him ...

To Noxx!

● ● ●

"I'm really not sure we should be coming back here," said Ruby, when the boat pulled up at the jetty on Intrepid Island.

"I need to tell Chancellor Rex what happened," Jack said. "About Danny."

Ruby's orange eyes glistened for a moment, but she blinked the tears away. "I hope he can help," she said quietly.

After leaving his parents safely at their apartment, Jack had used Hawk to contact Ruby. She and Ellie had been the first students to make it to the museum without being spotted, so they were hanging around waiting for the others to show up.

It had taken the best part of an hour to tell his mum and dad the truth about Hero Academy. Obviously, they couldn't believe it at first, despite what they'd been through themselves. Then their shock had turned to anger at the danger Jack was being thrust into. But they were also proud. His mum had wanted him to stay at home, out of trouble. But there was no way he could do that while Danny was lost in Noxx, and General Gore was free to open more portals.

I'm the Chosen One, Jack thought, as he and Ruby took the lift up to the cliffs where Hero Academy stood. *It's up to me.*

The school courtyard was eerily silent. All the other students were still in Ventura City, though Jack knew they were sure to be back soon, when the word got out that the Noxx spy had been found and the danger from the stolen shadow vial had passed.

Jack's heart throbbed. Danny had been the first to welcome him to Hero Academy. Even when the shadows had transformed him, he'd used the last of his strength to fight on the side of good. Jack shuddered to think where he might be now. Raptrix was terrifying enough, but he was nothing compared to the cruelty of General Gore.

As they walked along the

battlements, Chancellor Rex appeared at the other end. Behind him came the other teachers who'd stayed on the island.

"Jack? Ruby?" the Chancellor said in surprise, eyeing the Shadow Sword. "What are you doing back here? You know all students must stay away until we have identified the spy."

"It was Danny," said Ruby.

The blood drained from Chancellor Rex's face.

"The portal shadows touched him," said Jack. "General Gore was controlling him all along."

The Chancellor took a step back,

hand going to his mouth. "And to think … Oh, I've been a fool."

"Why?" said Jack.

Chancellor Rex lowered his hand. "My visions showed me a boy from the academy going to Gore," he said. "I thought it was … *you*."

The air shimmered beside them, and Ms Steel appeared. "I saw a Hero Academy boat leaving Ventura City," she said sternly. "I know there must be a good reason you've returned."

Jack took a deep breath. "In a way, your vision was right, Chancellor," he said.

The headmaster frowned. "How so?"

"Because I *am* going to Noxx," said Jack. "Not because a shadow is controlling me, though — I'm going because I must rescue my friend."

Chancellor Rex sighed. "If Danny has gone there, I'm afraid he is lost."

But Jack wasn't going to back down. "Danny saved my parents," he said. "I won't leave him there."

"And Jack isn't going alone," said Ruby, her face hard.

The Chancellor glanced at Ms Steel and she shook her head. "No human has ever ventured to the realm of Noxx and lived to return," he said. "I cannot allow you to go."

"But—" Jack began.

Ms Steel put one hand on his shoulder, and one on Ruby's. "Your courage is admirable, but what you ask is impossible. Put all thoughts of it from your minds. Danny is lost — for ever."

Jack looked into the courtyard below, at the old portal and the fossilised remains of Noxxian soldiers. He could not accept that Danny was just another casualty of the ancient war.

He realised Ruby was looking in the same direction. As he caught her eye, she nodded, and he knew she wasn't ready to give up either.

"You're right," he said to Ms Steel and the Chancellor. "It's just so hard, because he was our friend."

The Chancellor offered a sympathetic smile. "He will be remembered here always," he said. He turned to Ms Steel. "Let's arrange for the rest of the students to return," he said. "We must make plans. General Gore will not stop until he has taken this world and made it his."

He strode away, followed by the other teachers. With a last, sad look at Jack and Ruby, Ms Steel vanished.

The two friends found themselves alone on the battlements.

"What's the plan?" asked Ruby.

Jack looked down at the frozen portal. A thousand years had passed since that epic battle, but another war was fast approaching. And if he was the Chosen One, the fate of everyone was in his hands.

He knew what they must do. "We're going to Noxx," he said.

VENTURA WAS A VILLAGE THEN, ON THE
SITE WHERE VENTURA CITY STANDS
TODAY. GRETCHEN GATHERED A GROUP OF
WARRIORS TO TAKE ON GENERAL GORE
AND HIS FORCES. ONE WARRIOR WAS
FROM THE DESERT REALM OF (SOLUS)
ANOTHER FROM THE UNDERWA...
SEQUANA, AND MANY ... OF
AROUND THE ...
HAD S...

they soon wo
entura, a you
the power of
the site where
d a group
rces. One
other from
other
owers,
a secret
ese

TIMETABLE

MON	TUE	WED	THUR	FRI
ASSEMBLY	ASSEMBLY	ASSEMBLY	ASSEMBLY	ASSEMBLY
POWERS	POWERS	POWERS	POWERS	POWERS
COMBAT	STRATEGY	TECH	COMBAT	STRATEGY
MATHS	GEOGRAPHY	ENGLISH	HISTORY	ENGLISH
HISTORY	SCIENCE	MATHS	SCIENCE	GEOGRAPHY

LUNCH!

				WEAPON TRAINING
TECH	COMBAT	COMBAT	STRATEGY	GYM
GYM	GYM	WEAPON TRAINING	GYM	HOMEWORK
GYM	GYM	GYM	GYM	FREE
HOMEWORK	HOMEWORK	HOMEWORK	HOMEWORK	

13.00
14.00
15.00
16.00

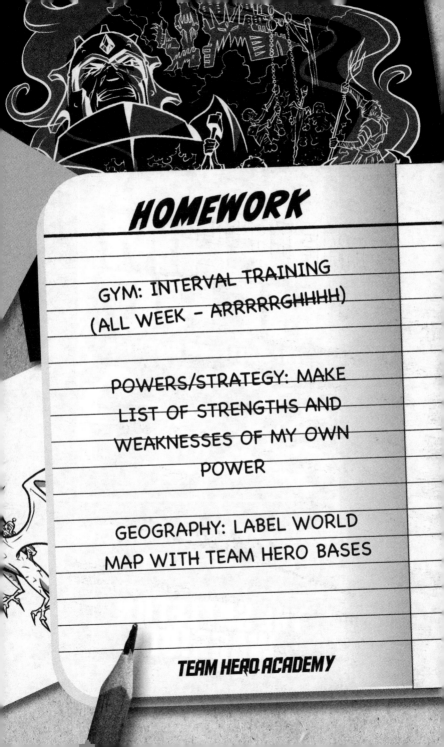

READ ON FOR A SNEAK
PEEK AT BOOK 4:

THE SKELETON
WARRIOR

CHAPTER 1

THE PORTAL ORB

We join the story in the technology lab, where Jack and Ruby are searching for a portal generator that can take them to the underground world of Noxx ...

JACK SPOTTED a grey ball sitting beside a broken computer screen and went over to it.

"That thing?" said Ruby. "It looks like an old football."

On closer inspection, Jack saw that

its metal surface glowed softly. He reached to pick it up.

"I strongly recommend you don't touch it!" Hawk said in alarm. "It's a Portal Orb. My analysis shows it's never been used before."

"It's our only chance to save Danny," Jack said, "we have to try …" There was a small switch on the top. Jack pressed it and the orb hummed. Its surface swirled with dazzling colour.

"Wow," breathed Jack. He put his hand to it — and felt a powerful force pulse up his arm. "I think it'll work if you just touch it! Quickly!"

Ruby put her hand next to his. The

humming grew louder. She raised her voice over the noise, "How will it know we want to go to Noxx?"

Immediately, the lab lurched from under Jack's feet. There was a flash of light, and a falling sensation, like he was going down a roller coaster.

"I think it understood you!" Jack shouted, but his words were snatched away by a roaring wind.

Then there was nothing but darkness. Jack heard Ruby shouting something, but she seemed very far away. He fell down, down, down ...

CHECK OUT BOOK FOUR:
THE SKELETON WARRIOR
to find out what happens next!

WIN AN ADVENTURE PARTY AT GO APE TREE TOP JUNIOR*

WITH

How would you like to win an epic party at Go Ape! for you and five of your friends?

You'll get up to an hour of climbing, canopy exploring, trail blazing and obstacles and a certificate to take away too!

The Go Ape! leafy hangouts are the perfect place to get together for loads of fun and prove that you've got what it takes to be the ultimate hero.

For your chance to win, just go to

TEAMHEROBOOKS.CO.UK

and tell us the names of the evil creatures that feature in the four different Team Hero books.

Closing date 31st October 2017

IN EVERY BOOK OF
TEAM HERO SERIES
ONE there is a special
Power Token. Collect
all four tokens to get
an exclusive Team Hero
Club pack. The pack
contains everything you and
your friends need to form your
very own Team Hero Club.

MEMBERSHIP CARDS • MEMBERSHIP CERTIFICATE • STICKERS • POWER GAME • BOOKMARKS

Just fill in the form below, send it in with your four tokens
and we'll send you your Team Hero Club Pack.

SEND TO: Team Hero Club Pack Offer, Hachette Children's Books,
Marketing Department, Carmelite House, 50 Victoria Embankment,
London, EC4Y 0DZ.

CLOSING DATE: 31st December 2017

WWW.TEAMHEROBOOKS.CO.UK

ease complete using capital letters *(UK and Republic of Ireland residents only)*

RST NAME

JRNAME

ATE OF BIRTH

DDRESS LINE 1

DDRESS LINE 2

DDRESS LINE 3

OSTCODE

RENT OR GUARDIAN'S EMAIL

I'd like to receive Team Hero email newsletters and information about
other great Hachette Children's Group offers (I can unsubscribe at any time)

*Terms and conditions apply. For full terms and conditions please go to
teamherobooks.co.uk/terms*

*TEAM HERO Club packs
available while stocks last.
Terms and conditions apply.*

FROM THE BESTSELLING AUTHOR OF BeastQuest

ADAM BLADE

TEAM HERO

LAIR OF THE FIRE LIZARD

SPECIAL BUMPER BOOK

FIND THIS SPECIAL
BUMPER BOOK ON SHELVES
FROM OCTOBER 2017

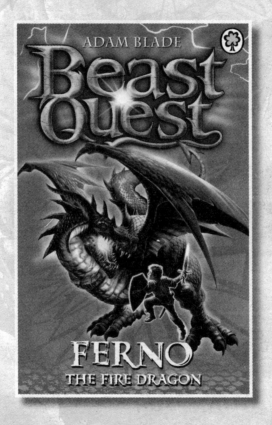

Go Ape!
TREE TOP JUNIOR

BIRTHDAY PARTIES

at 18 locations UK wide

PARTY BAGS PARTY ROOMS T-SHIRTS

Find out more at goape.co.uk
or call 0845 094 8813†